History of Photography

Contents   **Page**

written by Barry Holden

Many years ago, there were no photographs. If people wanted a picture of someone or something special, they would pay an artist to make a painting.

The first cameras were invented about two hundred years ago. There were box cameras and folding cameras that could only take one photo at a time.

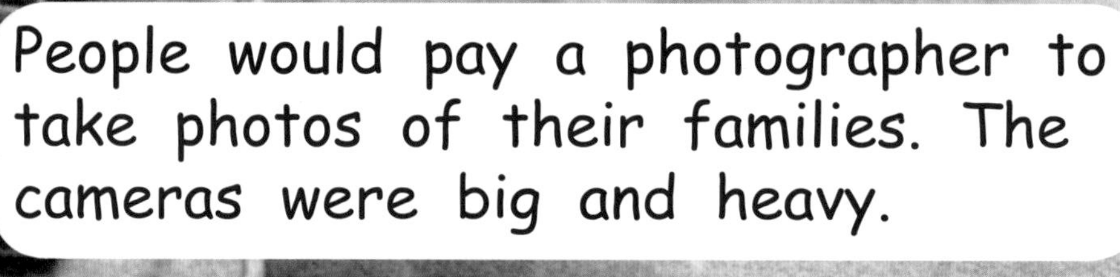
People would pay a photographer to take photos of their families. The cameras were big and heavy.

4

The photographer had to put a large, black cloth, like a tent, over his head and camera to keep out the light.
photographer

After a long time, smaller cameras were made. They had rolls of film that took many photos.

People got these new cameras to take their own photos. They could be printed, but only in black and white.

Movie cameras with black and white film were invented about a hundred years ago. These first films had no sound, so they were called "silent movies".

People would pay to watch them at a theater, with a piano playing music. These movies were very jumpy, so people called them "the Flicks".

Much later, sound was put on the films. Then they were called "talking pictures" or "the talkies". There were lots of theaters where people could watch these movies.

The next good thing was color film, which made the pictures look more real.

Most families had a camera to take their own photographs. They would keep photos in a special book called an album.

Some people got movie cameras to make their own films. People would take pictures of their children and friends having fun. These films were called "home movies".

Television was invented more than fifty years ago. Now TV cameras take photos of things all over the world. We stay at home to watch the news and our favorite programs.

Photography is used everywhere. Astronauts took photos on the moon, and robots send back photos from space. Divers use special cameras to take pictures underwater.

Most mobile phones have a camera. Take your phone from your pocket to make a call or — click! Smile for the camera! That's another photo for your album.